USS *Constellation*

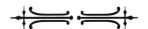

A boatswain's mate from the USS Constellation

USS
Constellation
Pride of the American Navy

BY WALTER DEAN MYERS

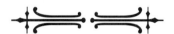

Holiday House / New York

Acknowledgments

The author would like to thank Nancy Bloom,
board member of the USS *Constellation*,
Will Eisner of the Eisner comic book studio,
and Bill McAllen, photographer,
for their help on this project.

Text copyright © 2004 by Walter Dean Myers
All Rights Reserved
Printed in the United States of America
www.holidayhouse.com
First Edition
1   3   5   7   9   10   8   6   4   2

Library of Congress Cataloging-in-Publication Data

Myers, Walter Dean, 1937–
USS *Constellation* / by Walter Dean Myers.
p. cm.
Includes bibliographical references and index.
ISBN 0-8234-1816-2 (hardcover)
1. *Constellation* (Frigate)—History. I. Title: *Constellation*.
II. Title.
VA65.C683M94 2004
359.8'32'0973—dc22   2003056764

To Linda Trice,
my friend and writing buddy

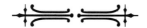

Contents

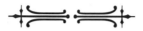

USS *Constellation*

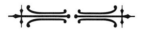

The USS Constellation, *as it looked in 1802*

1. The First *Constellation*

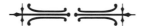

When in the Course of human events, it becomes necessary for one people to dissolve the political bands which have connected them with another, and to assume among the Powers of the earth, the separate and equal station to which the Laws of Nature and of Nature's God entitle them, a decent respect to the opinions of mankind requires that they should declare the causes which impel them to the separation.

S O BEGINS the Declaration of Independence, a document that led to the creation of the United States of America. On the 4th of July 1776, the thirteen American colonies formally declared their intention to break away from the powerful British empire. The signers of the Declaration understood that King George III would not allow the colonies simply to secede. There was no doubt that Great Britain would go to war against its colonies, as the king had already stated in a proclamation of 1775:

All our officers, civil and military, are obliged to exert their utmost endeavours to suppress such rebellion, and to bring the traitors to justice.

King George's position was clear. He would defend the right of Great Britain to keep its American colonies by force. The Declaration of Independence therefore was also a commitment by the colonies to war against Great Britain.

The thirteen colonies were populated by white colonists, free and enslaved blacks, and Native Americans. The whites were, of course, British subjects. Thousands of troops, also British, were stationed in America at that time. When the Declaration of Independence was announced in Philadelphia, these troops were ready to maintain order and put down any armed rebellion. The colonists had already raised an army of their own and had chosen as its leader a wealthy planter from Virginia by the name of George Washington.

The strength of the British army lay in its experience, discipline, and highly trained officers. The British also had excellent weapons, as well as the most powerful navy in the world. British officers thought that the inexperienced Americans would be incapable of standing against the might of the British empire.

But the colonies had advantages as well. The unfair tax burden placed on the Americans served as a unifying force, something the British public lacked. Also, the colonists were traditionally hunters. This experience of stalking a prey and shooting was an advantage in combat. Another advantage lay in the American rifle, slower to load but more accurate than the British musket. A nation of hunters and shooters with experience fighting in the French and Indian wars made the colonists formidible opponents.

But the war would not be fought only on land. The colonies depended heavily on their ability to keep their harbors open to trade. Boston, New York, Philadelphia, Charleston, and Savannah were all busy ports into which ships brought tons of merchandise both from American cities and from Europe. Once the "rebels," as they were called by the British, announced their intentions, all ships trading with America were considered to be enemy vessels. British ships began stopping, boarding, and taking away their goods as war bounty.

While the young country could seek volunteer soldiers from among the farmers and city dwellers of the colonies, it had no navy. The newly formed American government responded to this need by issuing letters of marque. A letter of marque gave permission for a private ship to engage in combat with an enemy vessel and, if successful, capture any goods that the ship carried. It was a way to instant wealth, or instant death, depending on the outcome of the battle. These ships, not part of the regular navy, were called privateers. Anyone could apply for such a letter if he had the money to arm a ship, could find a crew willing to risk death for the chance to capture an enemy vessel, and was willing to pledge his allegiance to the United States.

Privateers played an important role in the American War of Independence. During this war, more than 1,500 privately armed American ships sailed the high seas. They harassed British shipping, captured some vital supplies, and put an additional burden on the Royal Navy.

A typical American privateer was the *Royal Louis*, which in 1781 sailed out of Philadelphia under the command of Stephen Decatur Sr. Among those on board was fourteen-year-old James Forten, a free black youth. The *Royal Louis* encountered the British vessel *Active*. The two ships began a desperate battle, with Decatur using his ability to maneuver a smaller ship to avoid the heavy guns of the British. Shots from the *Active* whistled through the air, tearing the rigging of the American ship and sending some of its crew members screaming to the deck.

But in the end it was the *Active* that received the most damage, finally unable to maneuver at all as her sails were ripped and masts broken. When the British ship lowered her flag in surrender, the Americans cheered wildly. Decatur commanded the ship into port at Philadelphia to the delight of the townspeople. The British ship was stripped of all her valuables, and the proceeds were divided among the crew and the owner of the American ship.

Young Forten would not always be so fortunate. On the *Royal Louis*'s next voyage, the sturdy ship and her valiant crew were captured. Forten spent the rest of the war on the notorious British prison ship the *Jersey*.

The War of Independence lasted from 1775 to 1781. During this time, it became clear that the British would not defeat the Americans. They had to send their army thousands of miles across the Atlantic by ship, while at the same time fighting the French, who had sent their own ships to intercept the steady stream of British vessels headed toward America. The Treaty of Paris, signed in 1783, formally recognized the United States of America as an independent country.

When the War of Independence ended, the newly born nation began the process of creating a national government. It was not an easy task. Some

The old Jersey—*a notorious British prison ship*

people wanted a king, as they had been used to under British rule. Some wanted to end slavery in the United States immediately, while others wanted to maintain the practice. The colonists were in the unique position of consciously creating a new nation. Everything they were doing in search of a perfect system of government became a symbolic as well as a practical way of representing themselves. The Liberty Bell in Philadelphia, the Declaration of Independence, the American bald eagle —all became important national symbols.

When delegates from the colonies gathered in Philadelphia in 1787 to draw up the Constitution of the United States of America, they considered not only how they wanted to be governed but also what problems the new nation might encounter. One of the troubles they had already experienced was piracy on the high seas.

The American merchant vessels were part of a long British seafaring tradition. When the colonies broke away, they represented a loss of one-third of the entire British commercial sea trade. For the Americans, the ships were not only a way of doing business, but also a way of raising revenues for the government through import and export taxes. Yet British interference was not the only threat. Pirates were as well.

The delegates knew that the War of Independence might not have been won at all without the assistance of the French navy. There was much debate about creating an American navy. While the need for one seemed obvious, it was clear that the cost of building a navy was in itself a risk. A government that found itself in too much debt would be a government that flirted with disaster.

The American Constitution is based on the principle of separation of powers. Governing powers in the United States are divided among the three branches of government. The executive branch, or the president, has certain carefully defined powers. The judicial branch, headed by the Supreme Court, governs the legal system. The legislative branch, the Congress, makes laws and also has certain other duties. Two important duties assigned by the Constitution to Congress, and only to Congress, are the power to provide and maintain the armed forces, including a navy, and the power to declare war. In 1794, after much debate over the money involved, Congress decided to expand the sea power of the armed forces. There was no great enthusiasm to spend much on the project, however, and the government decided to buy a number of small ships from private owners in the meanwhile. Finally it was decided to build six frigates. The estimated cost would be a little more than $100,000 each.

A frigate is a fast, medium-sized ship designed for battle. Not as heavy or as well armed as some of the huge British ships with more than eighty guns, most American frigates carried between thirty-two and forty-two guns. But what they lacked in firepower they made up for with speed and daring.

Building a ship in the eighteenth century was a laborious task that allowed for few mistakes. The ships were made of wood. This wood had to be heavy enough and strong enough to withstand the rigors of the sea and to survive if the ship was in a battle, yet the ship had to be agile enough to sail swiftly through storms. Shipbuilders had to use the best wood available, which was generally considered to be that of the live oak tree. The live oak tree was found only in the southeastern United States and the Spanish Gulf Coast. Its density and resistance to rot and parasite infestation made it especially useful in ship construction. The natural curves of the live oak were used to minimize excessive bending, which would weaken the wood. Good, solid wood could last for decades.

George Washington made the final selection of names for the six proposed frigates: the *Constitution,* the *United States,* the *Constellation,* the *President,* the *Chesapeake,* and the *Congress.* The *Constellation* was supposedly named for the configuration of stars on the American flag, representing the joining of the states into one nation. The first three ships constructed were the *Constitution,* built in Boston; the *United States,* built in Philadelphia; and the *Constellation,* built in Baltimore. The main purpose of the ships was to defeat the pirates. Once a pact with the states supporting the pirates had been worked out, construction was halted.

The *Constellation*'s deck would be 164 feet long. Its beam, or width, would be 40 feet, 6 inches wide; and its huge masts would rise more than twelve stories high.

Thomas Truxtun, who had commanded a privateer during the Revolutionary War, would oversee the ship's construction and be her first captain. The ship's keel, the lumber under the center of the ship that forms the "backbone" of a vessel, was laid in 1795; and in September 1797, the completed ship was launched.

The Constellation
was launched in September 1797
from the port of
Baltimore, Maryland.

MARYLAND.   BALTIMORE, SEPT. 7.
FRIGATE LAUNCH.

" This morning, precisely at 9 o'clock, at the navy-yard of Mr. STODDARD, the builder, was launched, the United States Frigate CONSTELLATION.—The novelty of the scene (she being the first frigate ever built at this port) drew forth an immense concourse of citizens, of both sexes, and of all ages, and notwithstanding the earliness of the hour appointed for the launch, the number, we are warranted in saying, was never equalled on any occasion in this city. The surface of the *Patapsco* was covered with innumerable boats, and the adjacent hills east of *Harris's creek,* swarmed with spectators ; and so admirable too were the situations around, that every one had the pleasure of gratifying his curiosity, without risking the least accident.

" A number of volunteers, in uniform, were admitted on board, while others were set to guard the yard and permit no one to enter, unless engaged in the business of the day. The workmen, amounting to 200, being thus kept unobstructed, carried on there work with such regularity and dispatch, as reflected the greatest credit both on themselves and their able conductor. Every order was communicated by a ruffle from the drum, and the operations of the men in wedging up the vessel, &c. were apparently performed with as much exactness and precision, as the manual exercise by a regiment of veterans.

" The anxious moment now arrived—and now description is beggared. Every thing being in the most complete preparation—all the blocks taken away, every man from under the vessel, and the hull standing on almost nothing but the slippery tallow, orders were given for knocking away the last staunchion ;—This being done, she moved gracefully and majestically down her ways, amidst the silent amazement of thousands of spectators, to her destined element, into which she plunged with such ease and safety, as to make the hills resound with reiterated bursts of joyful acclamations.

" Her plunge into the water was attended with so little velocity, that she came to anchor within 100 yards of the shore, and we can pronounce, from the authority of able and experienced judges, that no vessel was ever taken from the stocks in a more safe and judicious manner than the CONSTELLATION ; and that no man, on a similar occasion, ever acquitted himself with more honor and ability than did major BENJAMIN STODDER."

RHODE-ISLAND.

At her launching, the *Constellation* was a new ship for a new country. Piracy was common throughout the world, and prior to American independence, ships from the colonies had been protected by the British. This, of course, was no longer possible. America would have to defend itself. By then a new, and unexpected, foe had appeared. America's former ally France was engaged in a war with England as well as with several other European countries. The United States declared its neutrality and a desire to trade peacefully with both England and France. The French, however, rejected the claim of neutrality and began attacking American ships. In January 1797, the *Constellation*'s carpenter's mate, John Hoxse, described one such incident in which the American brig *Minerva* was taken.

> The privateer now hoisted French colors, and hailed us. We answered, from New York bound to Gibraltar. Then they lay right on board of us, and discharged a number of pistols, killing one of our men and wounding another very badly. After getting possession of our vessel, they went below, broke open all our trunks, and took every vestige of clothing from us, except what we had on our backs. They left us not even a chew of tobacco. They put a prize master on board of us, sheered off, and ordered us to be run into Algeciras.

This conflict between the two nations, although never officially declared a war, was deadly serious. Taking place entirely in a series of sea duels, the brief skirmishes against France were known as the Quasi War and were the first major test of the American fleet. The *Constellation*'s assignment was to escort American ships into the Caribbean. On February 9, 1799, the *Constellation* encountered the French frigate *Insurgente*.

The French had little respect for the young American navy and its lack of fighting experience on the high seas. The *Insurgente* was larger than the *Constellation* and had a hundred more men on board. The French captain,

Michel-Pierre Barreaut, knew there were two main ways of defeating an enemy sailing ship. You could shoot down her masts and sails so that the ship would not be able to maneuver, making her an easy target. This method, by keeping the hull, or body, of the ship intact, would also make her more valuable as a prize. A second strategy was to fire into the hull, killing as many of the ship's crew as possible so that she would surrender or burn at sea. The French wanted to take the American ship as a prize and so fired at her rigging.

The nimble *Constellation* maneuvered away from most of the shots and withstood those that tore through her canvas sails. Captain Truxtun had his gunners answer the *Insurgente*'s fire with a broadside. The *Constellation*'s heavy shells crashed into the hull of the French ship.

The French captain tried desperately to come as close to the American ship as possible so that his crew could board the *Constellation* and attack the Americans in hand-to-hand combat. Captain Truxtun saw Captain Barreaut's maneuvering and realized that if the French sailors reached the decks of the *Constellation,* the Americans would surely be defeated. But the men gathered on the deck of the *Insurgente* were also vulnerable.

Truxtun spun the *Constellation* so that she crossed directly in front of the French ship. The French guns, pointed from the sides of the ship, could reach few areas of the *Constellation* while the Americans unleashed a powerful broadside, raking the deck with shot. After more than an hour of point-blank firing and maneuvering, the French captain lowered his flag in surrender. It was the first victory for the official American navy.

Overleaf:
The USS Constellation *in pursuit of the French ship* Insurgente

The captors of the *Insurgente* were entitled to receive the following sums of money accruing from the prize: Captain Truxtun, $3,000; shared among the lieutenants and sailing master, $2,000; shared among the Marine officers, surgeon, purser, boatswain, gunner, carpenter, master's and surgeon's mates, captain's clerk, and clergyman, $2,000; among the boatswain's mate, gunner's mate, ship steward, sail maker, master-at-arms, armorer, and coxswain, $3,000; among the gunner's yeoman, quartermaster's mate, sergeant of Marines, drummer and fifer, and extra petty officers, $3,000; and shared among the seamen, ordinary seamen, Marines, and boys, $7,000—for a total reward of $20,000.

It was common to spread the news of major battles by making up songs about them, and the victory of the *Constellation* was soon being sung.

The Story of the United States Navy
The Constellation *and the* Insurgente
BY BENSON J. LOSSING

Come, all ye Yankee sailors, with swords and pikes advance,
'Tis time to try your courage, boys, and humble haughty France.
The sons of France our seas invade,
Destroy our commerce and our trade;
'Tis time the reck'ning should be paid
To brave Yankee boys.

On board the *Constellation* from Baltimore we came,
We had a bold commander, and Truxton was his name;
Our ship she mounted forty guns,
And on the main so swiftly runs,
To prove to France Columbia's sons
Are brave Yankee boys.

We sail'd to the West Indies in order to annoy
The invaders of our commerce, to burn, sink, and destroy.
Our *Constellation* shone so bright,
The Frenchmen could not bear the sight,
And away they scampered in a fright,
From brave Yankee boys.

'Twas on the ninth of February, at Montserrat we lay,
And there we spied the *Insurgente*, just at the break of day.
We raised the orange and the blue
To see if they the signals knew
The *Constellation* and her crew
Of brave Yankee boys.

All hands were call'd to quarters, and we pursued in chase,
With well-prim'd guns, our tompions out, and well splic'd the main-brace.
Soon to the French we did draw nigh,
Compell'd to fight, they were, or fly,
The word was passed, "Conquer or Die,"
My brave Yankee boys.

Loud our cannons thunder'd, with peals tremendous roar,
And death upon our bullets' wings that drenched their decks with gore;
The blood did from their scuppers run;
Their chief exclaimed, "We are undone!"
Their flag they struck, the battle won
By brave Yankee boys.

The *Constellation*'s next major battle would be in February 1800, when she encountered the French frigate *Vengeance* near the island of Guadeloupe, in the West Indies. The two ships fought from eight in the evening until one the next morning. F. M. Pitot, the French captain of the fifty-two-gun vessel, lowered his flag to surrender, but the *Constellation*'s masts were too badly damaged to take the larger ship as a prize and she escaped in the darkness.

The French reported losses of sixty dead and more than a hundred men wounded during the furious fight. The *Constellation* reported fourteen dead

U.S. FRIGATE

CONSTELLATION

FIGHTING SHIP with a FIGHTING HEART

THE INSPIRING STORY OF THE FIRST WARSHIP OF THE UNITED STATES NAVY

The young U.S. Navy routs the French warship Vengeance *in Will Eisner's comic book based on the* Constellation

and twenty-five wounded. One of the wounded was John Hoxse. Here he describes how he was injured:

> Towards the close of the action, as I was standing near the pumps, with a top maul in my right hand, with the arm extended, a shot from the enemy's ship entered the port near by, and took the arm off just above the elbow, leaving it hanging by my side by a small piece of skin; also wounding me very severely in the side, leaving my entrails all bare. I then took my arm in my left hand, and went below, into the cock-pit, and requested the surgeon to stop my bleeding, for my arm was already off.
>
> He accordingly stopped the effusion of blood, and I was laid aside among the dead and wounded, until my turn came to have my wounds dressed. The cock-pit at this time was full of the dead and dying, but I was so exhausted that I fell asleep, and was not sensible that any thing had happened, until I was called up to have my wounds examined and dressed. I was then taken up, laid on a table, my wounds washed clean, and my arm amputated and thrown overboard.

War at sea was a bloody business, whether it was against privateers or regular navy ships. Along the Barbary Coast of North Africa, pirates routinely preyed on merchant vessels. To avoid having a ship attacked by the Barbary pirates, as they were called, countries had to pay for protection. In 1815 the American government sent a small fleet of ships, including the *Constellation,* to the Barbary Coast to protect its ships. The force, led by Stephen Decatur Jr., not only freed American prisoners kidnapped by the pirates but also forced the leaders of the countries of North Africa, most notably Algiers, Tripoli, and Tunisia, to sign treaties with America promising to no longer attack its ships. On board the *Constellation,* in addition to her sailors, was a company of Marines. The "Marine Hymn" reflects their early experiences protecting Americans from the Barbary pirates: "From the halls of Montezuma, to the shores of Tripoli, we fight our country's battles in the air, on land, and sea. . . ."

An attack by Barbary pirates

"Showing the flag" is a phrase used to indicate that there is a national presence and a willingness to protect national interests. The *Constellation* and her outstanding officers, sailors, and marines "showed the flag" throughout the world from the early days of the Quasi War and helped to begin the American naval tradition.

Nothing is more beautiful than a sailing ship at sea on a clear day, her sails billowing in the wind as she cuts through the waves. But even as she sails in the calmest waters she is on a life-and-death struggle to survive the destructive forces of ocean travel.

A ship's wood has to be cared for carefully. Barnacles, small shelled animals, attach to ships and ship worms burrow into the wood and weaken it. The vessel's rolling motion over waves twists the boards, loosening her caulking and tar barriers. Every storm or heavy sea twists the ship in small ways, creating cracks that must be repaired and loosening joints that must be tightened.

A warship, such as the *Constellation*, suffers damage each time she goes into battle. Often the opportunity to repair the ship is limited, and emergency repairs further injure the vessel. Some of the damage done is obvious—a mast is splintered during a battle, sails are ripped, bulkheads are warped and come loose from their joints. Other damage, often deep within the structure of the ship, is less obvious, causing the sides to bulge or the keel to weaken. By 1854 the *Constellation*, some fifty-seven years old, was in poor shape. She had been altered a number of times, with her basic design being somewhat changed. The ship was taken to the Gosport Navy Yard in Virginia and put into storage.

At Gosport, construction began on a new ship. The shipbuilders probably took material that was available from other ships at the port. We know that some of the iron from the original *Constellation* was used as ballast for the newly constructed ship. It's possible that other parts were used as well, but we can't be sure.

But there was no doubt that the magnificent ship launched in 1854, bearing the proud name of *Constellation*, would continue the great naval tradition of the original frigate.

2. The Second *Constellation*

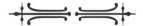

IN 1816, Congress authorized a massive warship construction program of liners and frigates for the navy. In each year after the bill was passed, the Congress would appropriate money specifically to pay for a part of that program with no allowance for any other new ships. It did, however, appropriate money for ship repair. In the 1820s, the navy found itself needing ships other than liners and heavy frigates and decided to get them by bringing in old ships for major repair, or "rebuilding." Sometimes the ship really received a major repair and came out with few outward changes, but outfitted for some new purpose. In other instances, about all that remained unchanged was the name. *Constellation* was the ninth and last ship involved in this kind of operation. Because this was officially called a "repair," the new ship would have to be a sailing vessel, even though steam power was coming into the navy at the time. Naval Constructor John Lenthall prepared the plans for a large ship-sloop, or corvette, armed with fewer but more modern weapons than those in the frigate that had been broken up. She would be the last all-sail warship designed for the U. S. Navy.

The USS Constellation, *now a sloop of war*

When the new *Constellation* was launched, August 26, 1854, she was armed with twenty modern guns on the gun deck, ten on the starboard side and ten on the port side, and two guns that could pivot, or turn, on the spar deck. In 1855, with a full crew of 20 officers, 235 sailors, and 44 Marines aboard, she was assigned to the Mediterranean fleet.

The crew of the *Constellation* worked in shifts, called watches, and had a variety of tasks to accomplish. The care of the ship was a major ongoing concern. A ship that had leaks, or whose sails were not in good shape, was in no condition to fight if she encountered an enemy or a storm at sea. Every part of the ship had to be in working order, every sail ready to be furled or unfurled at a moment's notice.

Lookouts were posted throughout the ship, peering along the horizon or into a gathering fog. The sails and rudder were constantly being adjusted to match the wind. In the event of a battle, sailors had to scamper up the masts to make repairs or adjustments. Gun crews had to know their jobs thoroughly, and keep the cannons ready at all times. If the ship was damaged, fires had to be extinguished and the wounded cared for. Marines served as sharpshooters, trying to pick off enemy sailors doing the same jobs as the crew of the *Constellation*. If a ship was boarded, the Marines were expected to be the first line of defense, and the sailors would fight with them to drive off the enemy.

The crew of a fighting ship was a carefully drilled team that had to perform its duties on a constant basis and keep the ship in condition so that she, too, could function at her best. Discipline and training were the keys to a ship's efficiency, and the crew of the beautiful *Constellation* underwent constant training for a series of captains to make sure that she was ready for any contingency.

The *Constellation* was named the flagship in 1859 and joined the African Squadron later in the year. Her captain was John S. Nicholas.

During the period immediately following the launching of the *Constellation,* there was only one major war, the Crimean War, and that did not involve the United States. The ship would soon, however, find herself in an unexpected conflict.

3. The *Constellation* and the African Slave Trade

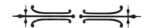

The Migration or Importation of such Persons as any of the States now existing shall think proper to admit, shall not be prohibited by the Congress prior to the Year one thousand eight hundred and eight, but a Tax or duty may be imposed on such Importation, not exceeding ten dollars for each Person.

——Constitution of the United States, Article I, Section 9

THIS SECTION of the United States Constitution refers to the slave trade; the "Importation of such Persons" means bringing people into the United States as slaves. As allowed by this section, Congress did pass a law saying that no slaves would be imported into the United States as of January 1, 1808. England had, by that time, also discontinued the slave trade, and so had Spain. Still, the trade, although illegal, continued. The reason was simple. A captured African could be bought for twenty to thirty dollars on the west coast of Africa and sold in the illegal slave trade markets in Cuba, South America, or the Caribbean for hundreds of dollars. Many adventurers were willing to take the chance of reaping huge profits in the slave trade, even if it meant facing trials and jail.

It was important to stop the trade in slaves at its source in Africa rather than in the United States or the Caribbean. If a ship was stopped at an American port, then the Africans would have to be transported back across the ocean to Africa.

As the United States Navy helped to battle the illegal importation of slaves into the country, the battle over slavery was becoming more heated within the United States. Southern states that supported slavery were becoming more and more suspicious of the Northern states, which seemed to be edging toward a complete abolition of the practice. So the *Constellation* sailed to Africa on a mission to stop the illegal slave trade abroad just as a national movement against slavery was growing at home.

The efforts to stop the slave trade faced many obstacles. Once the slave traders had Africans aboard, they would try to outrace the ships that were chasing them. If in danger of being caught, they would often try to gain

*Captain Andrew Foote led
the American slave interdiction.*

A boatswain's mate

some time by simply dumping their human cargo overboard, knowing that the pursuing ships would stop and rescue the Africans from drowning. All in all, it was a dangerous and cruel business.

It was fairly easy to tell the legal ships from the slavers. In the first place there weren't that many ships doing regular business in Africa in the 1850s. Merchant ships carried just enough men to handle the ship and just enough food and water to feed them. The rest of the space on the ship was devoted to cargo. The more cargo a ship carried, the more money it made. The sleeping quarters for the crew were small and cramped, with each man getting mere inches for his bedding. These quarters were usually in the forecastle, the front part of the ship. The captain of the vessel had a separate, roomier sleeping cabin at the stern, the rear of the ship.

When a ship was suspected of being a slaver, the first thing that was noted was the amount of provisions carried. If a large number of Africans were being transported across the ocean, a trip that usually took from thirty-five to fifty-five days, enough food and water had to be carried to feed them for the entire trip, even if the rations were spare. A more important consideration for the captain of the slave-carrying vessel was how to get air to the captives. If they were in the bottom of the vessel, away from fresh air, many would die from suffocation. On the other hand, the Africans couldn't be on the top deck because their very presence was illegal. To solve this problem, a new deck would be built just below the weather deck. There the poor souls being carried from their families could at least have the luxury of a few breaths of air as they lay in chains in the darkness.

American and British ships intercepting the slavers would, of course, look for actual persons chained aboard the ships. But even an empty ship with a slave deck and provisions would be confiscated.

After serving three years as the flagship of the Mediterranean Squadron, the *Constellation* had returned to the United States for a brief repair period. Then she headed for Africa, again as flagship of the squadron there. During her first year on station, she captured a ship called the *Delicia*. The presence of a slave deck told the crew of the *Constellation* all they needed to know, and the boat was confiscated. But the new *Constellation*'s biggest prize came nearly a year later. Wilburn Hall, a graduate of the Naval Academy and a twenty-one-year-old officer serving on the ship, wrote of his experience:

> The *Constellation* was cruising on the African coast, the men finding relaxation only at long intervals in a short rest at Madeira, or the Canaries; or perhaps at one of the islands in the Bight of Benin. After one of these cruises, when off the Ambriz River, near the Congo, in August 1860, the calm gave way to a refreshing breeze, and the *Constellation*, with all squaresail to royals, had just shaped her course for St. Paul de Loando. It was about 7 P.M., the sea was calm as a floor, and a beautiful moon lit the waters with a splendor rarely seen. The crew and officers were all on deck enjoying the refreshing change. Songs were heard forward, messenger boys were skylarking in the gangways, officers were pacing the lee quarter-deck. Suddenly from the foretopsail-yard rang out the cry, "Sail ho!"

Instantly laughter ceased, songs ended, men jumped to their feet—all was now expectancy. "Where away?" came sharply through the speaking-trumpet from the officer of the deck. "About one point for'ard of the weather beam, sir." Every eye caught the direction indicated. Sure enough, bright and glistening in the reflected moonlight, the sails of the stranger were seen, hull down, with the upper parts of the courses in view. She looked like a white phantom outlined against the clear-cut horizon. Glasses showed her to be a bark standing on the starboard tack, close-hauled to the wind, with every stitch of canvas drawing, royals, sky sails, and staysails. The *Constellation* was at this time on the port tack, with royals, running with the wind about abeam. In a moment came the order, "Lay aft to the braces! Brace sharp up! Down main-tack and -sheet! Haul the bowlines!" . . .

Soon the ship was dashing along on the star board tack with royals and stay-sails drawing. This evolution brought the chase on our weather beam. The *Constellation* was a remarkable sailer by the wind, and few ships were ever known to equal her when everything was braced sharp up and bowlines taut. The yards were now so sharp up that she ran nearer than the usual six points to the wind. In no long time the courses of the stranger began to rise, showing the gain we were making; and in an hour she was nearly hull up. It was as clear as day; but the light was that wonderfully soft light which the moon gives only in the tropics. The stranger's sails were as white in that light as a pocket-handkerchief. The breeze had freshened, so that we were running at least nine knots. Men had been sent aloft to wet down the topsails, and every thread was stretched with its duty, the leeches of the topsails just quivering.

At this time a gun from our weather-bow was fired—a signal for the stranger to heave to, but on she sped, silent as a dream. We could now plainly see through the glasses that there was not a light about the ship, a most significant sign. Another gun was fired. As the white smoke came pouring over our deck, we lost sight of the chase, but as it was swept to leeward, there she ran silent and glistening, with no tack or sheet started. Suspicion now amounted almost to a certainty that we had a slave-ship at hand. . . .

Our orders were to aim at her upper spars, as all were now convinced that the hull was filled with slaves.

But little did we know the spirit of the slave-captain. He had determined to take every chance for escape, even to the sinking of the ship. This he subsequently told me. He saw that we were beating him to windward. Suddenly he executed a movement which evinced the determination of the man. It was rash, perhaps because he lost ground; but he knew his vessel, and hoped by increased speed to prolong the chase, awaiting the chapter of accidents. . . .

The slaver was well on our starboard bow. Mr. Fairfax called me to go with him on the gun-deck, where we ran two heavy 32's out to, our bridle-ports ready for a chase dead ahead which soon occurred. I was directed to carry away the upper spars and rigging, and under no circumstances to hit the vessel's hull!

"Aim high and make your mark," he continued. . . .

Suddenly our attention was attracted by dark objects on the water ahead of us. The slaver was lightening ship by throwing overboard casks, spars, and even spare masts. The sea appeared as if filled with wreckage in a long line. All at once boats were seen. "They are filled with negroes," I heard some one cry on deck. "Steady on your course," I heard the flag-officer shout on the forecastle just above my head. Sure enough they were boats, and as we sped they seemed to be coming swift to us. My heart beat with quick emotion. I thought I saw them crowded with human forms. Men on deck shouted that they were crowded with people, out we swept by, passing them rapidly. The slaver hoped we would stop to pick up his boats, and thus gain more time, but his ruse made us even more eager. Now, our guns redoubled, we knew the end must come soon, but there seemed no way to stop the chase without sinking her, and humanity forbade a shot in her hull. Her captain realized the situation, but even then his courage was wonderful.

On we went. Suddenly I saw her course begin to change; she was coming to windward—her studdingsails came fluttering down, her skysails and royals were clewed up, her foresail also, and as she rounded up to the wind and backed her maintopsail, the *Constellation* had barely time to get in her canvas, and round under her maintopsail, scarcely two hundred yards to windward.

"Away there, first cutters, away!" called the boatswain's mates, as their shrill whistles ceased.

I had barely time to get on deck, after the guns had been secured, before I saw the first cutter, one of the small boats we carried, with our gallant first-lieutenant himself as the boarding officer, speeding like an arrow to the vessel, her oars scattering sparkling diamonds of phosphorescent water as they rose and fell. Every officer and man was leaning over our low hammock-rails, breathlessly waiting and watching. We saw the cutter round up to the gangway.

Fairfax's active figure could be seen quickly mounting the side, and then he disappeared as he leaped over the gangway into the ship we had captured. For two or three minutes the stillness was painful. One could hear men breathing in their excited anxiety. Suddenly there was a hail, in tones which I can recall as if heard to-day-clear, distinct, and manly, *"Constellation,* ahoy! You have captured a prize with over seven hundred slaves." . . .

The slaves were nearly all on the slave-deck, shouting and screaming in terror and anxiety. I leaned over the main hatchway holding a lantern, and the writhing mass of humanity, with their cries and struggles, can only be compared in one's mind to the horrors of hell as pictured in former days. But I paid dearly for that sight. The sickening stench of hundreds of naked beings crowded into a space so small, in so warm a climate, without ventilation, was frightful. Overcome by horror at the sight and smell, I turned faint and sick at heart and hastened to the stern.

The *Cora,* here reported as having been seized with a fresh cargo of slaves on board, was recorded, as follows in the list of slavers published in the *Evening Post* of July 28: "No. 19, Bark *Cora,* 431 tons, Latham from New York. Cleared by master. Owned at Havana. Vessel detained and discharged. Allowed to sail under bonds."

The *Cora* was detained under examination at this port from May 19th, 1860, until she was allowed to sail on the 27th of June following. Her second clearance was granted, as had been the custom in previous cases where vessels were bonded. The *Cora* was bonded in the sum of $22,128 on the 23d of June, 1860. The bondsmen are Charles Newman of Brooklyn, and Robert Griffiths.

The captives rescued by the *Constellation* were taken to Liberia, a West African country created by the American Colonization Society to repatriate slaves who were freed in the United States.

Wilburn Hall went on to fight in America's Civil War—with the Confederate South.

4. The Making of a Sailor Aboard the *Constellation*

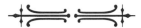

L IFE ABOARD a ship could be, and often was, very difficult. A sailor could be away from home for months, even years, at a time. The food often consisted of rock-hard bread, mashed and salted vegetables, and salted meats. The salt was used as a preservative. In Great Britain, which for years had been the largest naval power in the world, getting a full crew on a ship was at times so difficult that men would be kidnapped and dragged unwillingly to serve aboard vessels. Obtaining crew members for the American fleet, which was considerably smaller, was not as difficult, but the navy did find itself

"Hang on!"

The discharge papers of a black sailor, Thomas Bush,
at the end of the Civil War

> In 1837 Congress enacted that it would be lawful to enlist for the navy boys between the ages of 13 and 18 years, to serve until 21. With this authority a plan was speedily put in action, and shortly afterward the frigate Hudson had three hundred apprentices on board. The Secretary of the Navy, in his instruction to commanders of ships having boys on board, directed that they (the apprentices) were to be thoroughly instructed, so as to best qualify them to perform the duties of seamen and petty officers.

Excerpt from Our Naval Apprentice *magazine*

opening its ranks to a wide community of young men. The ships' list of personnel, called the muster roll, showed that in addition to whites, many blacks were enlisted in the navy, as well as citizens of other countries.

Once on board, the sailor had to live in cramped quarters, hanging his hammock between beams on the berthing deck. There was very little air circulating beneath the decks, and the smells were sometimes awful. In summer the berthing deck could be almost unbearably hot and in winter bitterly cold.

If the trip went exactly as planned, food supplies would be adequate, depending largely on foods that would not go bad without refrigeration, such as hard biscuits, potatoes, grains, and a variety of salted meats, often all cooked together. The officers fared somewhat better.

Young boys who wanted to join the navy could, with their parents' permission, enlist at thirteen years of age. Since few youngsters in the 1800s had proof of age, it was not uncommon for boys even younger to be part of a sailing crew. But merely joining a crew on a ship did not make them sailors.

The *Constellation* was a warship, part of the United States Navy. Wher-

Boys as young as thirteen
found their way onto the ships.

ever she went, she had to be self-sufficient. There was no time to return hundreds or even thousands of miles to pick up new personnel. The ship could be engaged in a battle at sea and lose many of her crew, but she would still, if possible, have to carry on. Each sailor had to be able to fill in where he was needed. There was much to learn.

Landsman was the rank given to the totally inexperienced adult sailor. He had everything to learn and was given the worst jobs on the ship. It was the landsman who did much of the cleaning, who learned how to pump out the bilges far below deck, who ran errands around the ship. And the first thing he had to learn was the names given to various parts of the ship.

Ships are laid out like small cities, except that the different parts of this city are stacked one over the other. The *Constellation*'s top deck—from which rose the masts, tall poles that held the rigging, spars, and sails—was called the spar deck. From this deck sailors on duty could lower, turn, or raise the sails, which caught the wind that propelled the ship. The wheel that was used to steer the ship by turning the rudder was here as well. The helm, as it was called, was operated by two experienced sailors, four during battles.

To lift heavy items aboard the *Constellation*, a capstan was used. This was a simple machine, again on the spar deck, that rotated. Ropes were attached to the capstan and to the heavy object. There were holes in the capstan into which bars were placed. The crew pushed on the bars, which turned the capstan and lifted the weight.

An all-sail ship is driven only by the wind. The ship's captain or another senior officer tells the men what he wants done with the many sails: which sails should be furled [rolled up so that they don't catch the wind] or unfurled, and how they should be positioned. Each crew member working the sails has to know exactly how to handle them. The sails are moved by ropes [called sheets]. Each rope on a ship, and there are miles of them on a large ship such as the *Constellation,* has a specific name and location. When the ship has to maneuver quickly, the officer in charge calls out his orders quickly, referring to bowlines and tacks and sheets. Each sailor has to know exactly what is meant, which rope has to be tightened or loosened, and which sail has to be tied or unfurled. In the 1800s, an experienced sailor was said to "know the ropes."

Sailors were also expected to identify the ships they saw. Frigates were

Young recruits flocked into the service.

always warships with three masts, many sails, and as many as forty-eight guns. A schooner had two masts, and a sloop one. The second *Constellation* was a sloop of war, with three masts and her main guns on one deck.

From the position of landsman, with experience, a sailor could become an ordinary seaman. The next step up, again with more experience, was seaman, and the next level was that of petty officer. Petty officers took charge of the other crew members and saw that the ship ran smoothly and according to the wishes of the ship's officers.

Below the spar deck was the gun deck, where the cannons were kept, always clean, polished, and ready for action. They were fastened onto heavy bases and tied in place, and they were fired through gun ports along the sides of the ship. When it was time to fire a cannon, it was pulled back from the porthole and swabbed out to remove any powder residue from a previous firing. A powder charge, securely wrapped in sacking, would be brought up from a room two decks below and tamped down into the barrel of the cannon. Then a ball, often weighing as much as 100 pounds or more, would be placed into the mouth of the cannon, and it, too, would be securely pushed into the rear of the cannon. The charge would be lit from a hole in the top rear of the cannon. The deafening explosion could send the projectile to targets more than a half mile away.

The title page of an 1873 instruction manual

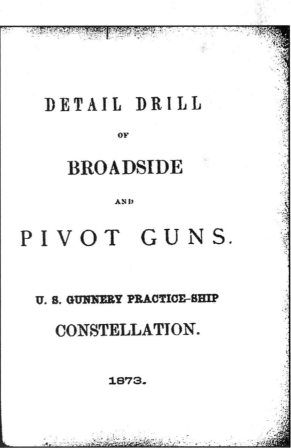

DETAIL DRILL

OF

BROADSIDE

AND

PIVOT GUNS.

U. S. GUNNERY PRACTICE-SHIP

CONSTELLATION.

1873.

There could also be a shower of sparks from the cannon, which explains why each firing would depend on bringing a powder charge to the gun from belowdecks. It clearly wouldn't do to have the powder kept in the same area as the exploding cannons. Also, a cannon that wasn't properly tied down would react to the explosion that sent the shot off. Such "loose cannons" could accidentally kill crew members or do serious damage to the ship.

Often, smaller men or young boys would perform the dangerous task of carrying the powder from the lower deck to the gunners. They had to be quick, small enough to maneuver the narrow spaces belowdecks, and brave. The boys carrying the powder from deck to deck were called powder monkeys. In a battle, the scarves they wore around their necks would be quickly fastened around their heads to cover their ears, because the sound from the huge cannons going off could break their eardrums. The boys would work in bare feet to remove the possibility of a spark from a nail in a shoe.

During the heat of battle there was always the possibility of the ship being damaged by enemy fire. But a far more dangerous possibility would be that, in the excitement, the ship's store of powder would accidentally be ignited by her own crew. The powder was kept in compartments called magazines. Although the magazine was well below the waterline, such an accident would almost surely be the end of the ship and most of the crew. Once stored aboard a ship, a candle's flame through a small window in an adjacent room provided the only light. The instructions for handling the powder give a good idea of just how dangerous it was:

Precautions to be observed in handling gunpowder, in moving or transporting it, and, in stowing the Magazine.

In transporting powder or ammunition from the Magazines on shore to the powder boat, the utmost care must be taken that the tanks and boxes are carefully

A young powder monkey

handled, and not allowed to be dragged over the ground; when a tank or loaded shell is placed on the ground or deck, that it is done with as little shock as possible.

Before the Magazine is opened, the lights in light room or box must be lighted, and while it is open, smoking is not permitted, all galley and other fires are extinguished, and all lights put out, except those, designated for this duty.

The Corporal, with the entire detail for lights and fires, will be held responsible for the strict observance of these rules.

Powder and ammunition will be received through the nearest port to the Magazine. The passages and the deck between the Magazine and the port must be covered with swabs or mats.

The powder-tanks and shells must be carried to their respective rooms with bearers, and set down with care on mats or swabs.

Before stowing the tanks, the exteriors are to be carefully cleaned, and the lids examined; no tools of any description are to be used, except those made of copper or wood.

Every person, before entering the Magazine, should be searched by the Gunner or his mate; all inflammable material of any kind, all objects made of iron or steel, such as knives, or keys, &c, must be placed in charge of the sentry; he must, then take off his shoes, and will then be permitted to enter the passages, where he puts on the Magazine dress and shoes.

Care must be taken that there is always a supply of fresh water, either led by a pipe from a tank on deck next above, or in covered, wooden cans or in buckets in the Magazine passage, and also damp swabs at hand; water being both for drinking purposes and to extinguish any local fire which might be caused during an action from the passage of an enemy's shell through the Magazine passage.

All hammering or coopering in the Magazine is forbidden.

DUTIES OF THE MEN ENGAGED IN PASSING POWDER.

As soon as the drum beats to quarters for action, the men detailed for the Magazine passages are first, to place the fire tubs, and are then to repair to the scuttle, where they will be searched, and will take off their shoes; they will then enter the passage.

It is also highly important that the men who are stationed at the scuttles over the passage shall immediately after the entry into the Magazine of the people stationed there, replace both hatches to the Magazine.

The men stationed in the passage take the passing-boxes as soon as filled, and pass them up on deck through the passing-scuttle. Passing-boxes will receive one charge for heavy guns, and two charges for light guns.

The men behind the screen are so divided that one half look out for the full boxes, and the other the empty ones.

The runner boys stationed at the bottom of the chutes receive the empty boxes from the chutes on damp swabs, strike them over the fire tubs filled with water so that all grains of powder that may have remained in the box will have fallen into the water before the box is passed to receive another charge.

Those detailed to handle the full boxes receive them from the Magazine scuttle, and pass them through the flap in the screen to the carriers.

The utmost silence must be preserved in the Magazine and passages; no loud talking is to be allowed under any circumstances; care must be taken that the Magazine doors are kept closed.

MAGAZINE PROPER

As soon as the signal "Clear ship for Action" has been sounded, the men detailed for the Magazine will, as soon as searched, enter the passage, put on their dresses and shoes, and will enter the Magazine as soon as the Corporal [detailed for Magazine duty] has received word that the Magazine lights are lit.

They will close the doors after them, and will open the smaller ones for passing the charges. The Gunner or his mate opens only as many tanks as are immediately required, one for distant firing and one for ordinary firing.

The men stationed at the small scuttles in the doors are to receive the cartridges, and pass them up to the men behind the screen, who pass them through the hole to the man who fills the empty boxes in front of the screen, and are to be careful to pass word to the Gunner or his mate whenever there is a change to be made in the charges. As soon as one tank is empty another must be opened.

The strictest silence must be observed and good order must prevail in the Magazine, and with all persons in the powder-division, as in the event of battle everything depends upon the rapid supply of powder and projectiles to the battery.

Light Rooms

As soon as the beat "Clear ship for Action" is sounded, the lights in the light rooms will be lit by the man detailed for that purpose. As soon as the candles are lit he will report the same to the Gunner or his mate in charge of the Magazine, and to the Officer commanding the powder division. He will remain in the vicinity and constantly examine the lights that they may burn brightly and clearly.

After every person has left the Magazine, and it has been closed, he will extinguish the lights in the light room.

Shell Rooms

The general duties of the men in the shell-rooms are much the same as those in the magazine. The projectiles must be passed with the greatest possible rapidity, and silence must be preserved.

Passing Charges

Upon the beat, "Clear ship for Action," the men detailed to pass powder place the screens before the scuttles, open the scuttles, secure the chutes for passing the empty passing-boxes, and, as soon as possible, receive the full boxes from the Magazine passage, and pass them on deck. Both the supply and return scuttles are to be used for the first supply of powder.

Handling the powder belowdecks in the dimly lit and stuffy hot areas where the powder was stored was a dangerous but vital part of any battle. And all the while these boys or men were below, handing up powder and shot to the gunners, there would be some enemy ship somewhere trying to send a ball into the ship's powder to destroy them. If the ship were boarded and hand-to-hand fighting broke out, the captain might order the magazine to be protected, perhaps by flooding it with water, to prevent the powder from being taken by the enemy.

Below the gun deck was the berthing deck. The crew lived here, with officers in fairly comfortable quarters toward the stern of the ship and the crew forward. Each noncommissioned crew member had a space in which he hung his hammock at night. Half of the *Constellation*'s crew was on duty at a time. When the half that was sleeping was awakened, they rolled up their hammocks, came up to the spar deck, and put the hammocks in racks around the side of the ship. The rolled-up hammocks were out of the way and also served as part of the ship's defenses. Of course, when the ship was in a battle, all hands were on deck or at their battle stations.

The berthing deck was where the crew ate and where they spent much of their leisure time. The officer's quarters and the wardroom, where the officers met to plan the ship's strategy or perform other administrative duties, were also on the berthing deck.

Below the berthing deck was the orlop deck. This was the lowest usable deck on the ship. It was often divided into sections. A sick bay, for wounded or sick crew members, was here, as was a brig, or jail. Below this deck was cargo space, where the ship's supplies of food, water, and spare parts were carried. The magazine was on this level as well. And at the bottom of the ship was the bilge. Water from the decks above drained into the bilge and had to be pumped out on a regular basis.

The endless chores, carried out in weekly and daily routines, were interrupted only with equally endless training drills. Mistakes in the drills were often punished more severely than misbehavior. Discipline on a ship such as the *Constellation* was strict. The running of the ship depended on the absolute cooperation of all sailors. In battles, the ability of the ship to survive depended on the swiftness with which she could maneuver. A ship that could outmaneuver her enemy could place herself in a position from which her guns could fire effectively while the enemy's guns could not. And the abil-

Up the ropes
on the Constellation

Even young sailors could specialize; this petty officer's field was engineering.

ity to maneuver depended on the skill of the captain and the response of his men. One man who did not perform his job immediately when told to do so might cause the ship to be lost.

A sailor that posed a discipline problem could be placed on light punishment, which might mean extra work. He could be given brig time, jailed, or limited to "bread and water." Before 1850, he could have been tied down and actually whipped.

Sailors, whether they were young boys or old hands, soon came to understand that the quality of their lives depended on a very high degree of cooperation, with every man on board knowing his job, along with as many other jobs as possible. A sudden storm at sea could capsize a ship. A lucky shot from an enemy ship could endanger the ship and everyone aboard. In such extreme cases, the safety of the ship and her crew depended on the ability of the officers and men to handle the ship expertly and bravely.

Training drills were conducted on a regular basis, with the captain noting every response to his orders. When sailors weren't fighting an enemy, they spent much of their time training or keeping the ship in top condition. On the *Constellation*, a wooden ship, the wood had to be inspected constantly for rotting. Sails had to be kept in tip-top shape. The miles of rope that controlled the sails and spars had to be kept in excellent condition, with "loose ends" checked for fraying.

Cleanliness was a major concern on ships. Any contagious illness among the three hundred or so men could spread quickly and wreck the efficiency of a fighting crew. Sailors were inspected for neatness and cleanliness despite the difficulty of keeping clean. Fresh water was often not available, and sailors had to clean themselves as best they could.

But without a doubt, the most valuable quality that a sailor could have was personal toughness. The sea was unforgiving. A sailing vessel that foundered in a storm or did not respond well in a battle could cause the death of everyone aboard. The old hands knew what to expect of the life of a sailor; young boys quickly learned.

A boatswain's mate

The sloop of war defends the Union.

5. The Civil War

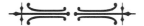

THE DIFFERENCES between the Northern states, with their growing industrial might, and the agricultural South were clear. In the late 1850s, the South was experiencing an economic boom based on cotton production. Many Southern politicians and landowners felt that the Southern states would be better off as a separate country. Abraham Lincoln, the president of the United States, was considered to be against slavery and, therefore, against Southern interests. But the South could not prevent his election in 1860, and this heightened the tension between the Northern and Southern states. South Carolina was the first state to secede from the union, and it was in South Carolina, at Fort Sumter, that the Civil War began, on April 12, 1861.

The *Constellation* was still cruising off the coast of Africa on her mission to stop the slave trade. In May the sloop of war spotted a suspicious ship and closed on her. The ship was the *Triton*, an American slaver. The *Triton* had no slaves aboard but was clearly outfitted for the slave trade, and the *Constellation* claimed her as a prize. But when the *Constellation*'s officers boarded the

Triton, they were surprised to discover that the ship's crew considered themselves prisoners of war. The officers of the *Triton* claimed allegiance to the Southern states, known as the Confederacy, and believed themselves to be surrendering to a ship of another nation, the United States. The officers of the *Constellation* soon learned that there was a war and that they had captured an enemy ship.

The outbreak of the Civil War found the *Constellation* in a strange position. She was one of the newer ships of the United States Navy, but she was a ship propelled completely by sail. Steam-driven ships were the latest technology. Nowhere was this more evident than in the famous battle between the *Monitor* and the *Merrimack* on March 9, 1862, which proved that the age of wooden warships was over.

A key element of Union war strategy was to blockade Southern ports so that the agricultural South could not trade for needed arms and supplies. To this end, the Union, which had many more ships than the South, set up walls of warships to prevent foreign ships from entering Southern ports and Confederate ships from leaving. One such wall was established at Hampton Roads, Virginia. But the Confederacy had come up with an answer to Union naval superiority. It had raised a sunken ship, the USS *Merrimack,* and had built on her hull what amounted to a miniature fortress—a heavily armored, twenty-gun structure whose plating was composed of four inches of iron. The vessel had been renamed the *Virginia.*

When the *Virginia* arrived at Hampton Roads on March 8, she was met by a wall of five Union ships: the frigates *Congress* and *Cumberland* and three smaller frigates, the *St. Lawrence,* the *Minnesota,* and the *Roanoke.* The *Minnesota* and the *Roanoke* carried small steam engines to augment their sails, but the *Congress, Cumberland,* and *St. Lawrence* were, like the *Constellation,* all-sail vessels made of wood.

The *Congress* spotted the strange Confederate ship first and prepared for battle. The frigate prepared her guns, sighted her target, and fired when the *Virginia* was a quarter mile away. The Union sailors watched as their shots bounced off the low vessel steaming in their direction. The return fire ripped through the crew of the *Congress,* sending wounded and dying men to the deck. There was no wind, so the *Congress* was helpless as the *Virginia* passed her and headed toward the *Cumberland.*

The *Virginia* steamed toward the *Cumberland* and took the first volley, the shells bouncing harmlessly off her iron hull. The front of the *Virginia* was shaped to ram into the weaker wooden ships, and she headed for the vulnerable

Both black and white sailors served on Civil War ships [1863].

side of the *Cumberland*. On board, the Union sailors fired again and again, to no avail. The *Virginia* smashed into the side of the *Cumberland*, at the same time firing her guns at point-blank range. Timbers splintered; cabins collapsed. Men were tumbling into the wide-open gaps created by the ramming. As the *Cumberland* began to burn and take on water, the *Virginia* reversed her engines and moved back to survey her work. Then, seeing that the *Cumberland* was done for, the *Virginia* turned her attention once again to the *Congress*.

The *Cumberland*, her decks covered with dead and dying men, had fought a gallant but wildly uneven battle.

The *Congress* prepared for battle. But it would be a battle against a ship that was steam-propelled and heavily armored. The gunners on the *Congress* fired away but knew, as their shots bounced off the Confederate ship, that it was useless. The *Virginia* raked the *Congress* with deadly fire, and soon the *Congress* lowered her flag in surrender. In less than two hours, one ship had dealt a huge defeat to the Union navy and forever influenced naval technology. It would remain the most devastating loss to the American navy until Pearl Harbor.

The Union had actually known about the Confederate ironclad and her whereabouts before the encounter at Hampton Roads. And it had been preparing its response: one of the strangest ships ever built, the USS *Monitor*. The ship sat low in the water and was little more than an iron turret housing two cannons. The turret had an advantage in that it could be turned to face in any direction, making aiming more efficient. The relatively shallow draft of the *Monitor* made her more maneuverable than the larger *Virginia*, and her armor was just as good. The *Monitor* was also steam driven.

The *Monitor* arrived at Hampton Roads on the night of March 8 and engaged the *Virginia* the next morning. The two ships circled each other and fired at nearly point-blank range, with neither being able to dent the armor of the other. The battle was a standoff in which both sides claimed victory.

The battle itself was awesome, with the heavy shells bouncing off the iron. Sailors in wooden ships knew their day had passed.

The *Constellation* could not hope to achieve victories against armored, steam-driven ships. But she did play an important role in the Civil War. The war was being fought mainly within the territorial borders of the United States. Both sides of the bloody conflict were also interested in world opinion. The Confederacy was convinced that if it won enough battles, it would gain the support of the European powers. It could buy ships from Europe, but because of international neutrality laws, the ships could not be outfitted for war. If the Confederacy bought a ship made in a foreign port, the ship would have to be unarmed until she reached North America. An all-sail ship, such as the *Constellation,* could effectively blockade any ship built in Europe and sent toward the Confederate navy. She could also protect American merchant vessels against Confederate raiders and serve as a training ship for young sailors. The *Constellation*'s assignments reflected all these duties:

Navy Department
February 28, 1862

SIR: As soon as the U.S. sloop of war *Constellation* is ready for sea, proceed with her with all practicable dispatch to the Mediterranean, touching on the way at the Azores, Lisbon, and Cadiz.

The main object in sending the *Constellation* to the Mediterranean is the protection of our commerce from the piratical depredations of vessels fitted out by those in rebellion against the United States. The principal one of these vessels, the *Sumter,* which has so far eluded our cruisers, when last heard from was in the vicinity of Gibraltar. Your chief duty will be the pursuit of that vessel should she remain in that quarter. At the same time, however, you will exercise vigilance in all cases.

On April 28, 1862, the *Constellation* was at Cádiz, Spain, patrolling that area on the lookout for Confederate vessels. Other areas she patrolled during the Civil War included the bay of La Spezia in Italy, and the Tunis coastline.

Throughout 1862 and 1863, the *Constellation* acted as a patrol vessel in the Mediterranean or wherever else she was needed. She also spent time at the Naval Academy, which had been removed to Newport, Rhode Island, for the duration of the war.

In December 1864, the *Constellation* went to Havana, where it was suspected that small Confederate vessels were resupplying. When it was seen that Havana was clear of rebel ships, the sloop of war returned to America.

The naval lessons of the Civil War had been clearly spelled out in the sea battles of Hampton Roads. At the end of the Civil War, the wooden, all-sail *Constellation* was retired from active combat and began a new phase of her career as a training and receiving ship.

6. A Training Ship

IN JANUARY 1865, the *Constellation*'s crew members whose enlistment periods had expired were discharged, and the rest of the crew was transferred to other ships. The *Constellation* served during the remainder of the war as a receiving ship, a housing accommodation for new sailors.

She continued in this role until 1869, when the question of what to do with her came up again. Merely to scuttle the fine old ship seemed a shame, but with a navy that needed men and officers trained to function on steam-driven vessels, the all-sail *Constellation* was clearly out of place. And yet unofficially it was recognized that the *Constellation* was more than just a ship. Through her multifaceted and storied career, the *Constellation* had become a symbol of American will to defend its democracy. And it was recognized that the new officers in the growing American navy could benefit from being exposed to this sense of history and of the American spirit.

The *Constellation* was made a training ship for the Naval Academy. Each summer the ship would unfurl her brilliant white sails and take another crew

Sailors aloft

The USS Constellation *in 1899*

of young officers to the Caribbean or across the Atlantic to Europe. For years, young naval officers aboard this historic ship learned navigation, seamanship, and the duties of an officer and a gentleman.

Modifications were made to the ship to assist in the training of young officers. The cannons were replaced to include a one-hundred-pounder [one

A 1908 postcard

hundred pounds being the weight of the shot!], as well as shell-firing guns, which were more accurate than the old ball-firing weapons. Storage spaces, once used exclusively for supplies on long voyages, were converted to accommodate the needs of a teaching facility. A navigating bridge was also installed.

The *Constellation*, as an important American icon, was also used for other purposes. In the late 1800s there was another devastating famine in Ireland. Much-needed funds and food were collected in America, and in March 1880, the *Constellation* carried more than 2,500 barrels of potatoes and flour to Ireland to ease the suffering in that country. The mission represented not only the efforts of Irish Americans and American charitable organizations to help save the starving people of Ireland, but also the willingness of the American government to be part of the humanitarian solution. Once again,

The Constellation *brings food supplies to Cork, Ireland.*

the *Constellation* was "showing the flag," expressing, as a symbol of America, the will of the people.

Following her trip to Ireland, the *Constellation* resumed her duties as a training ship. A young midshipman, E. C. Brady, described what it was like to be on the ship:

We were somewhat delayed in getting under way, as the Constellation had only the day before returned from Ireland. During one of the periodic famines there, she had been sent to the Emerald Isle filled to the gun-deck with "spuds" (potatoes).

Sailors learned to do whatever the navy needed.

For weeks we slept in an atmosphere of potatoes; we breathed potatoes, thought potatoes, and tasted potatoes, until the homely vegetable became loathsome to us before our return. . . .

Sometimes there wouldn't be enough fresh water for washing and we would have to use sea water. We were always given a moderate allowance of fresh water for teeth-cleaning purposes.

We had another source of supply in the *scuttlebutt*, a large wooden cask that stood on the main-deck filled with water for drinking purposes only. It used to be a regular thing to procure a bottle and draw water from it during the night for the next morning's wash, until someone put a guard on the scuttlebutt and we had to use seawater again. There was no way, of course, for taking a bath, unless overboard, or up on the forecastle when the night was dark. As it was usually cool at night-time, washing was a chilly performance.

Life for the young cadets aboard the *Constellation* was difficult. Some were discouraged by the rough life. Others were involved in accidents that ended their careers and, sometimes, even their lives. But those who survived the training cruises and the classes at the Naval Academy to become officers became a vital part of the American navy.

By 1910, however, the ship had outlived her usefulness. There were no more sails being made to replace her badly damaged ones, and the rigging was beyond repair. But three years later, the assistant secretary of the navy, Franklin D. Roosevelt, ordered the ship to be restored as an American relic.

Chief Petty Officers'

UNIFORMS

$10.00 — $12.00

AT THE

NEWPORT ONE PRICE

CLOTHING CO.,

208 Thames St.,   Newport, R. I.

*Sailors bought
their own uniforms.*

A boatswain's mate

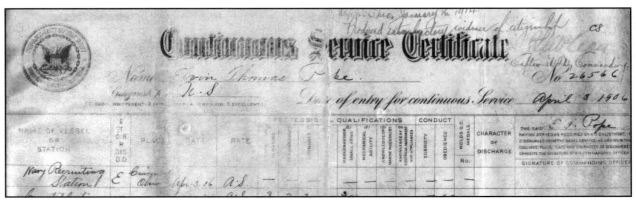

*Recruit Pope went
from recruit
to service on
the* Constellation.

*Landsman Pope's wallet,
which he carried
during his voyages.*

The Constellation *in its days as a training ship*

The ship was not fully restored. Many of the repairs were only cosmetic, to make the ship look reasonably good. The working capstans were replaced with one wooden capstan that did not work. Dummy sails were stuffed with straw to make them look windblown. At this time many people believed that the ship was the original frigate launched in 1797, so some of the modifications were ordered to make her look like the older frigate.

Throughout the life of the *Constellation,* she underwent a number of changes, according to the way she was being used. Decks were outfitted for the naval cadets, guns were removed or added, housing changes were made throughout the vessel. But old age and natural wear and tear had taken their toll, and the ship had to be towed to ceremonial appearances. In 1940, Franklin D. Roosevelt, then the president of the United States, had the ship commissioned once again, and in May 1941, had her designated as the relief flagship for the United States Atlantic Fleet, largely an honorary title. A flagship is the ship from which a fleet is controlled. The relief flagship is used in case the main flagship is being used for another purpose.

On December 7, 1941, the United States Navy at Pearl Harbor was attacked. The loss in human lives was great, but so was the loss of ships. All ships in fighting condition were mobilized in the emergency war effort. The *Augusta*, a heavy cruiser, and the flagship of the navy, was put out to sea. As the relief flagship of the Atlantic Fleet throughout World War II, the *Constellation* once again served her country.

7. Restoration

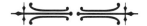

THE *Constellation* was so much a part of American history that in 1949 Congress passed a bill to restore the ship—as long as a substantial part of the money needed was publicly raised. In 1955 the ship was brought to Baltimore, Maryland. This was her historic home, where the first *Constellation* had been built and launched so many years before.

The raising of funds was difficult. The ship was seen by many as a mere museum piece. Adding to the difficulty was the growing controversy as to whether the ship, now badly deteriorating, was the original frigate launched in 1797. Or was she a completely new sloop of war built and launched in 1854? The backers of the original *Constellation* won, and there was an effort to restore the ship to her earliest configuration.

The restored *Constellation* was brought to Baltimore's Inner Harbor, where she was berthed through the 1980s. It was clear that once the ship had been restored, there was considerable interest in seeing her. The number of visitors began to approach a thousand a day, and the ship was clearly the centerpiece of the harbor. But over the years, the ship began to break down the

After World War II, the Constellation *was towed from Newport to Boston, where it was docked alongside the USS* Constitution

The dismasted Constellation *in 1953*

again, and in 1993 she was officially condemned by the navy. There were suggestions that the ship be taken out to sea and scuttled.

The *Constellation* Foundation, a group formed to save the ship, refused to give up. "Some things are worth fighting for!" became its slogan. Dedicated public officials, corporations, private citizens, the state of Maryland, and even schoolchildren rallied to raise the funds needed to restore the *Constellation* once more. In 1996 the ship was stripped and a multimillion-dollar rebuilding program began. Now the ship was considered to have been the

The Constellation *in 1980*

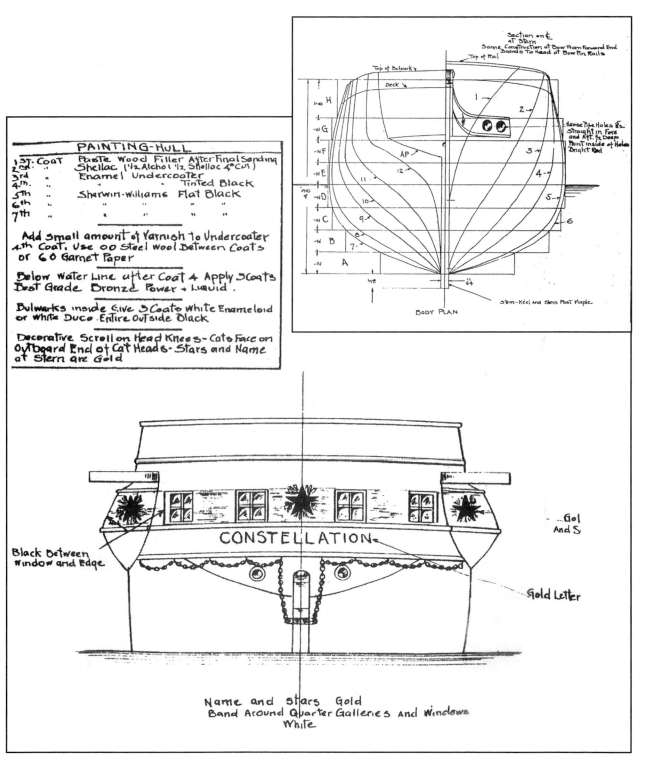

PAINTING-HULL

1st. Coat	Paste Wood Filler After Final Sanding
2nd. "	Shellac (½ Alchol ½ Shellac 4" Cut)
3rd. "	Enamel Undercoater
4th. "	Tinted Black
5th. "	Sherwin-Williams Flat Black
6th. "	" " "
7th. "	" " "

Add small amount of Varnish to Undercoater
4th Coat. Use 00 steel wool between Coats
or 60 Garnet Paper

Below Water Line after Coat 4 Apply 3 Coats
Best Grade Bronze Power + Liquid.

Bulwarks inside Give 3 Coats White Enameloid
or White Duco. Entire Outside Black

Decorative Scroll on Head Knees - Cats Face on
Outboard End of Cat Heads - Stars and Name
at Stern are Gold

Black between
Window and Edge

CONSTELLATION

Gol
And S

Gold Letter

Name and Stars Gold
Band Around Quarter Galleries and Windows
White

Plans for ship's restoration

1854 sloop, and the rebuilding focused on the designs from that era. Fortunately, much of the ironwork from the 1854 sloop was being used as ballast in the ship's hold and could be restored. The ship was stripped down to her bare essentials and lovingly rebuilt. On July 2, 1999, the beautiful new *Constellation* was returned to Baltimore, where she is now docked.

Today, the *Constellation* Foundation, in conjunction with the Living Classrooms Foundation, brings thousands of schoolchildren onto the ship every year, allowing them an exciting and unique way of experiencing history and a hands-on approach to learning.

Tall and majestic, her masts towering over busy Baltimore Harbor, the *Constellation* still flies the flag proudly, a magnificent symbol of navy tradition and the American spirit.

The Constellation *today.*

Some Nautical Terms

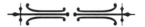

aft: the area from the middle of the ship to the rear of the ship; also, toward the stern

anchor: a heavy device, let down from the ship, to keep the ship from drifting when she's not sailing

ballast: heavy material put into the bottom of a ship to increase her stability

bark: a three-masted ship, with all fore and aft sails on the mizzenmasts

bilge: the lowest portion of the ship

boatswain's mate: an assistant to the boatswain, who is responsible for the boats, sails, and rigging, and also for summoning the crew

bow: the front end of a ship

bowline: a rope running forward from the edge of a sail, used to keep that edge taut

bulwarks: the raised "wall" around the spar deck

capstan: a device for moving or raising heavy weights

course: the direction a ship is heading

even keel: when a ship floats level in the water

forward: toward the bow of the ship

frigate: a three-masted warship with one covered gun deck, capable of carrying 28 to 44 guns

hatch: an opening in the decks

head: the ship's toilets

helm: the ship's steering wheel

"INITIATED"

"I GOT MINE"- CROSSING THE EQUATOR

In a seafaring tradition, sailors were sometimes tossed overboard the first time they crossed the equator.

jib: a triangular sail at the front of a ship

keel: the backbone of the ship

lee: the direction away from the wind

mainmast: the middle and highest mast on a three-masted ship. The *Constellation*'s mainmast is 170 feet high.

Marine: a soldier who is assigned to a naval operation. The *Constellation* usually had forty to fifty Marines assigned to her.

masts: the poles that hold the sails

midships: the middle of the ship

mizzenmast: the mast behind the mainmast

ordinary : a ship awaiting repair

orlop: the lowest usable deck, not a full deck running the length of the ship

outboard: outside

port: the left side of a ship when facing the bow

ports: the holes in the sides of a ship. They could be air ports, gun ports, etc.

royal: the sail above the topgallant sail. To "set to royals" means to unfurl and rig most of the sails, for maximum speed.

scuppers: the holes in the sides of a ship that allow water from waves or rain to fall back into the sea

sheet: the rope leading aft from each lower corner of a square sail used to control the way it is set

ships of the line: a three-masted warship with two or more gun decks, capable of carrying 64 to 100 guns *sloops of war:* a three-masted warship that carried her 20 to 26 guns on the open upper deck

spar deck: the uppermost deck in an American warship

spars: round timbers rising from the top deck

starboard: the right side of a ship when facing the bow

The USS Constellation

stern: the rear of a ship

swabs: a mop, or "swabbie" for sailors

tack: rope leading forward from each lower corner of a sail used to control the way it is set; also to change course by turning into and across the wind

wake: the trail of water behind a ship

wardroom: the living area of commissioned officers

wear: to change course by turning away from the wind

Selected Bibliography

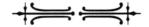

Books

Abbot, Willis J. *The Naval History of the United States*. New York: Dodd, Mead and Company, 1890.

Bobb, Lawrence J. *Sailor Life Aboard the USS* Constellation. Westminster, Md.: Opera House, Inc., 1999.

Chappelle, Howard, and Leon D. Polland, *The* Constellation *Question*. Washington, D.C.: Smithsonian Institution Press, 1970.

Foote, Andrew H. *Africa and the American Flag*. New York: D. Appleton & Co., 1854.

Gruppe, Henry E. *The Frigates*. Chicago: Time Life Books, 1979.

Hand, Susan Train. *John Train and Some of His Descendants; especially Charles Jackson Train, USN*. New York: n.p., 1933. Privately printed.

Hoxse, John. *The Yankee Tar: An Authentic Narrative of the Voyages and Hardships of John Hoxse and the Cruises of the U.S. Frigate* Constellation. Northampton, Mass.: John Metcalf, 1840. Printed for the author.

King, Cecil. *Atlantic Charter*. New York: Studio Publication, 1943.

Lossing, Benson J. *The Story of the United States Navy*. New York: Harper & Brothers, 1881.

Miller, Francis Trevelyan. *The Photographic History of the Civil War:* Part 6, *The Navies*. n.p.

Williams, Glenn F. *USS* Constellation*: A Short History*. Virginia Beach, Va.: Donning Company, 2000.

Wines, E. C. *Two Years and a Half in the Navy: Journal of a Cruise in the Mediterranean and Levant on Board U.S. Frigate* Constellation, *1829—1831*. Philadelphia: Caret and Lee, 1832.

Periodicals

Columbian Centinel [Boston, Mass.]. [16 September 1797].

The Evening Post [New York]. [7 December 1860].

"The Negro in the Navy and Merchant Service, 1798—1860." *Journal of Negro History* [October 1967].

Newark Daily Advertiser [New Jersey]. [12 February 1842].

Our Naval Apprentice. [January-December 1902.]

Randolph, Evan. "Fouled Anchors? Foul Blow." *The American Neptune* [spring 1992].

"The Slave Trade in New York." *The Continental Monthly.*

Wegner, Dana. "An Apple and an Orange: Two *Constellation*s at Gosport, 1853—1855." *The American Neptune* [spring 1992].

Miscellaneous

Detail Drill of Broadside and Pivot Guns, U.S. Gunnery Practice—Ship Constellation. Washington, D.C.: Government Printing Office, 1873.

Divisional Course of Instruction, U.S. Gunnery Practice—Ship Constellation. Washington, D.C.: Government Printing Office, 1872.

National Archives and Records Administration. *Deck Logs, U.S.S.* Constellation 1855—1893. RG 45.

National Archives and Records Administration. *Muster Rolls, U.S. Navy Ships* 1862—1865. RG 24.

Sources

Those books, periodicals, or journals that were particularly valuable as sources of information and quotations for certain chapters appear below. All sources can be found in the Selected Bibliography.

Chapter 1: Abbot, *The Naval History of the United States; Columbian Centinel*; Hoxse, *The Yankee Tar;* Lossing, *The Story of the U.S. Navy*

Chapter 2: *American Neptune,* "An Apple and an Orange"

Chapter 3: *Continental Monthly,* "The Slave Trade in New York"; *The Evening Post;* Foote, *Africa and the American Flag*

Chapter 4: *Detail Drill of the Broadside and Pivot Guns; Divisional Course of Instruction;* Hand, *John Train and Some of His Descendants*

Chapter 5: Wines, *Two Years and a Half in the Navy*

Chapter 6: Hand, *John Train and Some of His Descendants*; *Our Naval Apprentice*

Chapter 7: *American Neptune,* "Fouled Anchors"

Websites

http://www.constellation.org
http://www.ussconstitution.navy.mil
http://www.history.navy.mil
http://www.archives.gov
http://www.mysticseaport.org
http://www.southstseaport.org
http://www.navy.mil
http://www.sdmaritime.org

Places to Visit

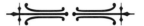

The USS *Constellation* Museum, Baltimore, MD   [410] 539-1797

The USS *Constitution* Museum, Boston, MA   [617] 426-1812

The US Naval Academy Museum, Annapolis, MD   [410] 293-2108

Time Lines

USS *Constellation*
Frigate
"Yankee Racehorse"

September 7, 1797	Is launched in Baltimore, Maryland
February 5, 1799	Captures the French frigate *Insurgente*
February 2, 1800	Defeats the French frigate *Vengeance*
1802–1803 1804–1805	Defends US interests against the Barbary pirates off the coast of North Africa
June 1813	Defends Norfolk, Virginia, from the British in the Battle of Craney Island during the War of 1812

1815–1819	Protects US trade in the Mediterranean
1840	Circumnavigates the world
1845–1853	In "ordinary" at Norfolk, Virginia
1853	Decommissioned and broken up at Gosford Naval Yard, Virginia

USS *Constellation*
Sloop of War

June 25, 1853	Keel laid
August 26, 1854	Is launched at Gosford Navy Yard, Virginia
July 28, 1855	Commissioned
1855–1858	Protects US trade in the Mediterranean
1859–1861	Prevents shipping of slaves; captures the slave ships *Delicia, Cora,* and *Triton*
1862–1864	Defends Union trade from Confederate raiders in the Mediterranean during Civil War
1864–1865	Serves on Union side during Civil War
1865–1866	Receiving ship, Norfolk Navy Yard, Virginia
1866–1868	Receiving ship, Philadelphia Navy Yard, Pennsylvania

1869–1893	Practice ship, US Naval Academy, Annapolis, Maryland
1894–1933	Stationary training ship, US Naval Training Center, Newport, Rhode Island
1933–1940	In "ordinary" at US Naval Training Center, Newport, Rhode Island
1941–1945	Relief flagship of US Atlantic Fleet
1946–1955	In "ordinary" at Boston Navy Yard, Massachusetts
November 17, 1996	Moved to drydock for restoration

Author's Note

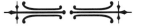

In my basement there are thousands of old photographs and bits of paper. These are ephemera, the unimportant papers that are not expected to last, such as theater tickets, newspapers, letters, and advertisements. Yet each item tells part of a story about some historical event or era.

History books, for example, may not tell us about blacks who served in the Union navy during the Civil War, but photographs do. Advertisements often tell us about the items people used in their daily lives. Even the size of the newspaper print may give us important clues as to what people of the time thought of a subject.

In researching the *Constellation,* I was lucky enough to find photographs once owned by a captain of that ship, the last all-sail ship built by the navy. Magazines from the naval training station in Rhode Island gave me an idea of what life was like for young sailors nearly a hundred years ago. A thin chapter in a training manual spoke volumes about the dangers aboard ship.

I love these old paper items, and the clues they provide to history. It makes research fascinating and helps the past come alive.

Illustration Credits

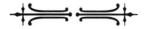

Front jacket and page 68: Copyright © 2002
Bill McAllen Photography

Pages 14 and 15: the Will Eisner studio

Page 65 and back jacket: US Naval Historical Center

All other illustrations in this book come
from the collection of Walter Dean Myers.

Index

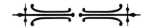

(Page numbers in *italics* refer to illustrations.)

training drills, 21, 42, 44

Treaty of Paris (1783), 4

Triton, 47–48

Truxtun, Thomas, 7, 9, 12

uniforms, *59*

United States, USS, 6, 7

United States of America:

    creation of national government in, 4–6

    national symbols of, *5*

U.S. Frigate Constellation (Eisner), *14, 15*

Vengeance, 13–16, *14, 15*

Virginia, 48–51

War of Independence, 1–4

    events leading to, 1–2

    naval warfare in, 2–4, *5*

wardroom, 41

Washington, George, 2, 6

water supplies, 44, *58–59*

whipping, 44

World War II, 62